I CAN WRITE THE WORLD

Joshunda Sanders

Illustrated by
Charly Palmer

SIX FOOT PRESS

HOUSTON • LOS ANGELES

The sun lights the sky over the Bronx
Bright orange and yellow
The smell of freshly baked bread in the air from the
Bakery up the street
The rattle of a fruit stand below

Rising up from the corner blow
Honking horns, salsa, and hip-hop music
The beeping of a truck that tows
My Bronx is a world of many colors and sounds
Shapes and sizes that are bright and bold

My name is Ava Murray
I am 8 years old

Mornings with Mommy include the news
Images and words I don't always catch
Views from the outside in
I think these are stories about my home
But how I feel and what I see don't always match

A girl about my age flashes on screen
It looks like adults are just being mean
She did something against the rules
Painting pretty pictures
That make plain walls sparkle like jewels

"Why is she in trouble?" I ask my Mom, Kim
"Because she made something pretty, but she
didn't ask for permission," Mom says
The art is called graffiti and it is one way
Kids who want to create
Share their talents with the world

"Creativity is using what you have
To make a map of your dreams
What you see in your mind
Or feel in your heart
Can come out in dance, colors, or beats"

When she was my age, there were no
Art classes at school
But Black and Brown kids taught themselves to
Move, sketch, rap, and made hip-hop culture cool

"Sometimes the way the world sees us
Is different from how we see ourselves," Mom says
She is talking about the news and its views

"See the frame around the window? It shapes
  Everything you see below
  Journalists on the news are
  Like the window frame," Mom says
"They tell the stories they think we should know"

Listening to Mom talk
Makes me imagine myself watching the Bronx
From the sidewalk
Talking to my neighbors
Typing up the stories I find everywhere I walk

At school, the thoughts and feelings still swirl
When we are asked to write about what we love
About where we live
I remember Mom's story and think,
"I can write the world"

"Can I interview you for my first story?" I ask Mom
"Of course, Ava. I'd be honored," she says
  Her face lighting up like sunshine
"Tell me more about the music and art you and your
  Classmates made"

At an old park, she says, "This is where it all began
With Grandmaster Flash and Kool Herc who made
New sounds from music with records and a
Microphone"

"Like a lot of our neighbors who are from islands
Like Puerto Rico or Haiti or Jamaica
When they came to the Bronx, they brought the
Sounds of their homelands: Salsa, reggae"

"Hip-hop music has all of that in it, too
Along with African drumbeats, Dancehall
Jazz, Rhythm & Blues"

She reminds me of the huge parties
In the summer on our block
With speakers so big the music makes
The whole Bronx rock
"Everything we make is connected to the past,"
Mom says. "It's how you make the art you love last"

"Long ago in Egypt, the first graffiti was made of
Symbols called hieroglyphics
The meaning of every mark, then and now,
Was tailored and specific"

When I tell the story of the Bronx I know and love
I share the story of art forms that traveled miles and
Years to get here
"Some stories about our home focus on the bad, not
The good," I say at the end

"But what is most beautiful in our world, what
Makes the Bronx stand out, may not always be
Understood"

What matters most is that we know we are
Connected to people who have always made the
Most of the world they were given
Making visible the beauty
That otherwise might be hidden

This is what journalists have always done
So I decide I will be one.
To be continued ...